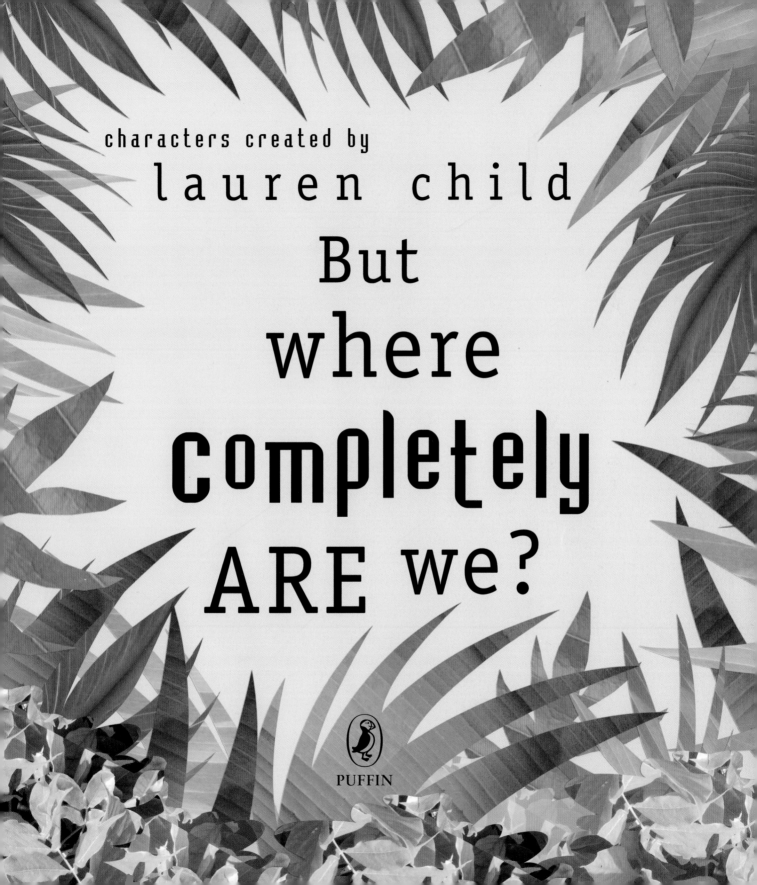

characters created by
lauren child

But
where
completely
ARE we?

PUFFIN

Text based on the script written by Samantha Hill

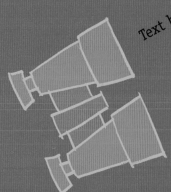

Illustrations from the TV animation produced by Tiger Aspect

PUFFIN BOOKS
Published by the Penguin Group: London, New York, Australia,
Canada, India, Ireland, New Zealand and South Africa
Penguin Books Ltd, Registered Offices: 80 Strand, London WC2R 0RL, England

puffinbooks.com

First published 2009
1 3 5 7 9 10 8 6 4 2
Made and printed in China
ISBN: 978-0-141-38477-1

I have this little sister Lola.
She is small and very funny.
Lola says, "I'm being a tent, Charlie.
Who lives in tents?"

I say,
"Explorers live in **tents**, when they go **exploring**."

"**Exploring**?" says Lola.
"Where do they go **exploring**?"

So I say,
"Well, they go
ALL over the world...

to hot deserts...

and
they
even
climb
whole
mountains
for the
very first
time."

"I would quite like to be an **explorer**," says Lola.
"Why don't we go now!"

So I say, "**Explorers** must always prepare properly."

"I know, Charlie. That's why I am taking
absolutely, completely
EVERYTHING...

just in case."

"But Lola, you have to choose carefully. We need...

a tent,

binoculars
for spotting
wild animals,

string for tying things,

a **notebook**
and
pen,

water,

food
and..."

"**Glitter!**" says Lola.
"In case we need
to do some
colouring
and sticking."

When we set off, Lola says,
        "Where are we GOING?"

And I say,
        "We're going
through blizzards...

and

tropical

rain...

" ... and we may even have to

wade through rivers.

"But we will keep on going and going…"

until we get there."

Lola says, "Where?

Where are we going?"

And I say, "Somewhere we can have a real adventure like..."

"... here!"

"But where completely ARE we?" says Lola.

"I think we must be in the
AMAZON RAINFOREST!
Look at all the
hundreds and
hundreds of trees."

We put up the **tent** and
then we have something to **drink**.

Lola finishes her drink
really, REALLY quickly.

And I say,
"Lola, you **can't** do that!
You always have
to save something
to **drink** in the **jungle**."

"That's OK, Charlie,"
says Lola.
"I told Mum I would
need lots of **pink milk** if
I was going **exploring**!"

But I say,
"You are NOT supposed
to bring extra supplies.
We are in a WILD and
faraway place remember
and we have to **forage**
for our **own** food."

"Oh, OK, Charlie –
I like **foraging**."

Later Lola says,
"Are there really bears
and tigers in the jungle?"

"Yes, Lola," I say.

So Lola says
"Could I just go upstairs
quickly and get Foxy?
I think he'd like the jungle
and he could protect us
from the tigers
and things."

"Lola, we CAN'T go home
when we are **exploring**.
Anyway, **explorers** don't
take **toys** on their adventures."

"Not even Foxy?"

Then it starts to **rain** and I say, "Wow! A proper RAINFOREST **storm.** We could be here for days!"

"Oh, I don't like it when it's **rainy**," says Lola.

"Mum said if it rained we could go back upstairs, Charlie."

"But real-life explorers don't go back upstairs."

And Lola says...

"I DEFINITELY
don't like
explorer camping.

It is wet and it is cold.
Can we just go INSIDE? Please?"

And then
    I had a
    REALLY
        good idea.

We go back
        inside...

... and soon we are
INDOOR-outdoor
camping!

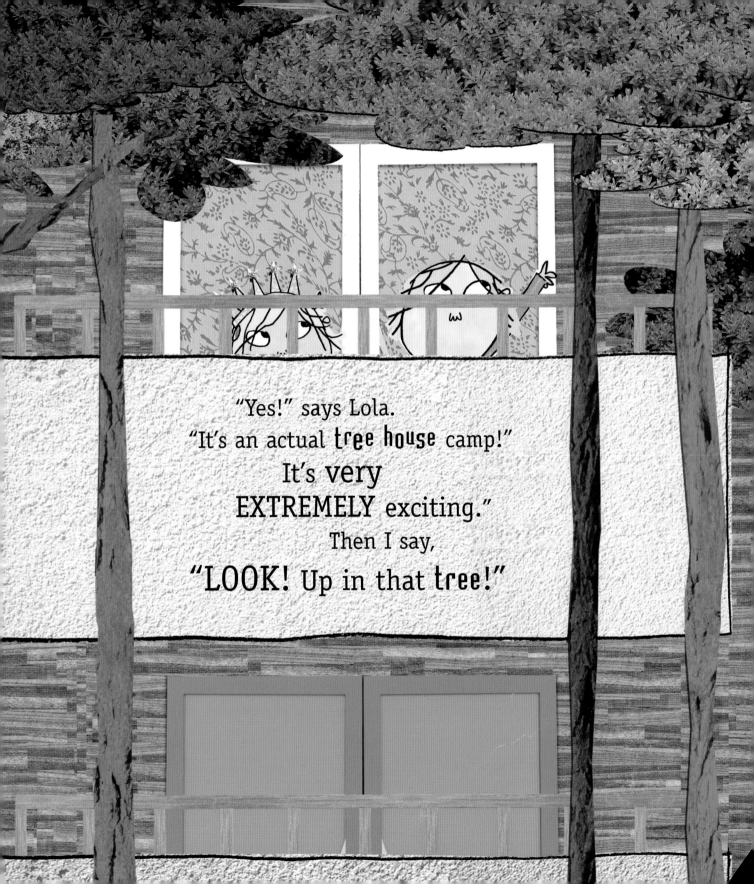

"Yes!" says Lola.
"It's an actual **tree house** camp!"
It's **very**
EXTREMELY exciting."
Then I say,
"LOOK! Up in that tree!"

"Tree frogs!"
I say.
"Hop on!
Follow me!"

"They are
funny
and
jumpy,"
says Lola.

Then we swing
through the **trees**.

"Weeeeeee, this is fun!" says Lola.

When we have finished **exploring**,
Lola says,
"We are **really** good **explorer-ers**,
aren't we, Charlie?"

And I say,
  "Yes, Lola,
    we **absolutely** are!"

Later, at our indoor-outdoor camp,
        I say, "Where are you going, Lola?"
And Lola says, "**foraging.**"
        "Foraging for what?" I say. "Giant coconuts?"
And Lola says, "No... **cheese!** From the fridge!"